T0198886

Flash Loves School

CharlieAlexander

Flash Loves School

Written by Charlie Alexander

Flash Loves School

Written by Charlie Alexander
Art Work by Charlie Alexander

Don't miss the bus Flash!

It was time to go to school.

It was nice to have a crossing guard!

Safety first!

"Here we are." said Flash.

It was a very big school.

The Pledge of Allegiance came first!

Flash saluted very proudly!

Flash really liked his new desk.

There was enough room for his legs.

It was time for math now.

Flash could add and subtract but division was still a little hard.

Flash enjoyed singing in the choir.

The sound of voices filled the air.

It was time to put the books in the library.

Flash carried a big stack of books.

Flash loved his painting class!

He liked every color.

In gymnastics, Flash climbed
the rope.

It was pretty high.

It was time for recess.

Flash tried riding his friends bike.

Flash had fun on the swing.

So did his new friend!

So much fun with friends.

Flash was enjoying his day at school.

Recess was nearly over.

The soccer game was in overtime.

Flash hurried to crash the cymbals.

Band class was the best!

Off to chemistry class next.

Flash was careful not to spill the beaker.

Studying geography was making Flash hungry!

It was almost time for lunch!

The lunch line was long.

But it moved quickly.

French class was right after lunch.

Bonjour Madam!

It was time for pottery.

Flash was busy shaping a ceramic vase!

The principal was handing
out report cards.

Flash made the Honor Role!

Flash was asked to clap the

erasers.

They were full of chalk dust!

Studying the stars was fascinating!

Flash loved looking through the telescope!

The custodian made sure the school was very clean!

He was using his favorite mop!

Flash helped his friend to
find the nurse.

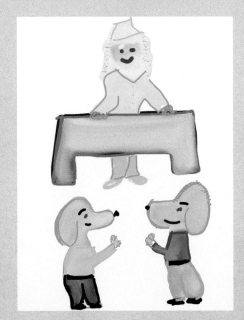

It's no fun to feel sick.

Robots were the last adventure before graduation.

The robots seemed to be aware of it!

Flash was receiving his diploma.

What an exciting day!

Flash has graduated!

Congratulations Flash!

Flash was very surprised to be asked to the class dance.

A surprised look made his face look funny!

It was the school dance! The band was awesome!

Everyone was dancing! Even Flash.

Flash addressed the whole class.

The end

(It's really just the beginning.)

Charlie Alexander

Flash goes to school and graduates with high honors. He writes on the blackboard and learns to spell. Math is one of Flash's favorite subjects. Of course, Flash loves to have lunch in the cafeteria!

Charlie is a Jazz Pianist and Author of sixteen children's books. He lives in Ocala, Florida with his wife Becky and his pal Flash!

To order additional copies of this book, contact:
Xlibris
844-714-8691
www.Xlibris.com
Orders@Xlibris.com

Library of Congress Control Number: 2023905009
ISBN: 978-1-6698-7065-4 (sc)
ISBN: 978-1-6698-7066-1 (hc)
ISBN: 978-1-6698-7064-7 (e)

Print information available on the last page

Rev. date: 04/13/2023

Printed in the United States
by Baker & Taylor Publisher Services